♡

This book was
donated to the.
Hampden Family Center
on the day the
author visited the Children's
Bookstore and the children
visited with David McPhail.

Jen Hobbins
lovingly donated it to us.

May 17, 1997

Anne
Sledge

Warm Wishes to
All the Kids at
Hampden Family Center
from
David McPhail
May 17, 1997

Pig Pig
Gets
a Job

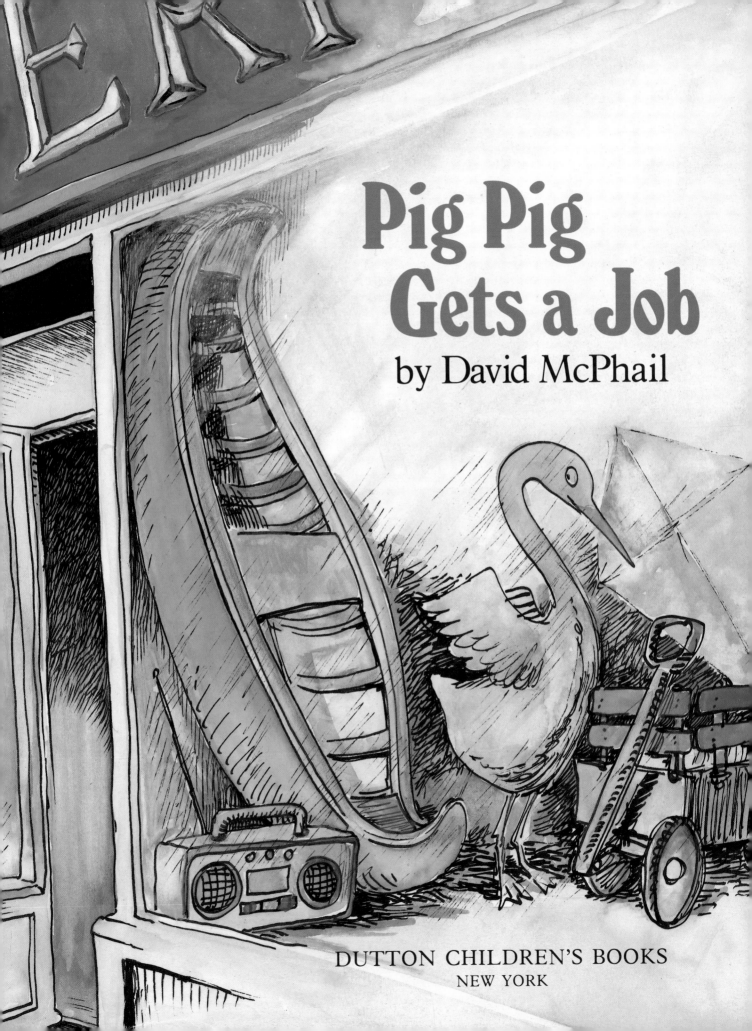

Pig Pig
Gets a Job

by David McPhail

DUTTON CHILDREN'S BOOKS
NEW YORK

to Pepe and Jeff
and enterprising youth everywhere

Library of Congress Cataloging-in-Publication Data
McPhail, David M.
    Pig Pig gets a job/by David McPhail.—1st ed.
        p.   cm.
    Summary: Pig Pig thinks of all the jobs he could get, from
cook to auto mechanic, and is enthusiastic about performing
similar tasks for his family at home.
    ISBN 0-525-44619-2
    [1. Pigs—Fiction.   2. Occupations—Fiction.]   I. Title.
PZ7.M2427Pgh   1990   89-25606
[E]—dc20   CIP
                                                          AC

Published in the United States by
Dutton Children's Books,
a division of Penguin Books USA Inc.

Designer: Nancy Goldenberg

Printed in Hong Kong by Wing King Tong Company Ltd
First Edition   10 9 8 7 6 5 4 3

One day after school, Pig Pig raced home
to make an announcement.

"I want some money," he told his mother.
"I want to buy something!"

"What do you want to buy, dear?" Pig Pig's mother asked.

"I don't know yet," Pig Pig answered, "but something!"

"And what will you do to get this money?" said his mother.

"Do?" said Pig Pig.

"Do," said his mother. "If you want some money, you must do something to earn it."

"Like work?" squealed Pig Pig. "Like a job?"

"Exactly like," said his mother. "Any ideas?"

Pig Pig thought for a moment.
"Well, I could be a cook!" he said. "I'm good at making mud pies!"

"You certainly are," his mother agreed, "but not everyone likes mud pies. Maybe you could fix some sandwiches for our lunch."

"I could get a job building houses!" said Pig Pig. "I could use the hammer and saw that I got for my birthday!"

"You might start with something small," suggested his mother. "A birdhouse would look nice in the yard."

"How about if I get a job as an auto mechanic!" said Pig Pig. "I could fix race cars when they break!"

"You could wash them and keep them shiny, too," his mother pointed out. "In fact, *our* car could stand a good cleaning."

"Or I could get a job at the dump," said Pig Pig, "picking up trash and crushing it!"

"Picking up your room would be good practice," urged his mother. "But please don't crush anything."

Pig Pig thought of yet another job.
"I could work in the circus," he said, "taking
care of the animals—training them and stuff."

"Stuff like feeding them?" Pig Pig's
mother asked. "And speaking of animals,
has Willie had his supper yet?"

"I have a great idea!" shouted Pig Pig.
"You could give me a job!"

"I could," his mother replied. "But what can you do?"

"Do?" cried Pig Pig. "Why, I can do plenty! I can feed Willie every day, and clean my room, and wash the car and fix it when it breaks down—"

"Washing it will be enough,"
interrupted his mother. "Is there
anything else?"

"There sure is!" Pig Pig went on.

"I can fix lunch sometimes,
and build things when we need them,

like a bookcase—or a birdhouse!"

"Splendid!" said Pig Pig's mother. "I could pay you, and you would have money to save or to buy something you want."

"And we could call all those things . . . my JOB!"
said Pig Pig proudly.
"We could," said his mother, "and we will!"

And they did.